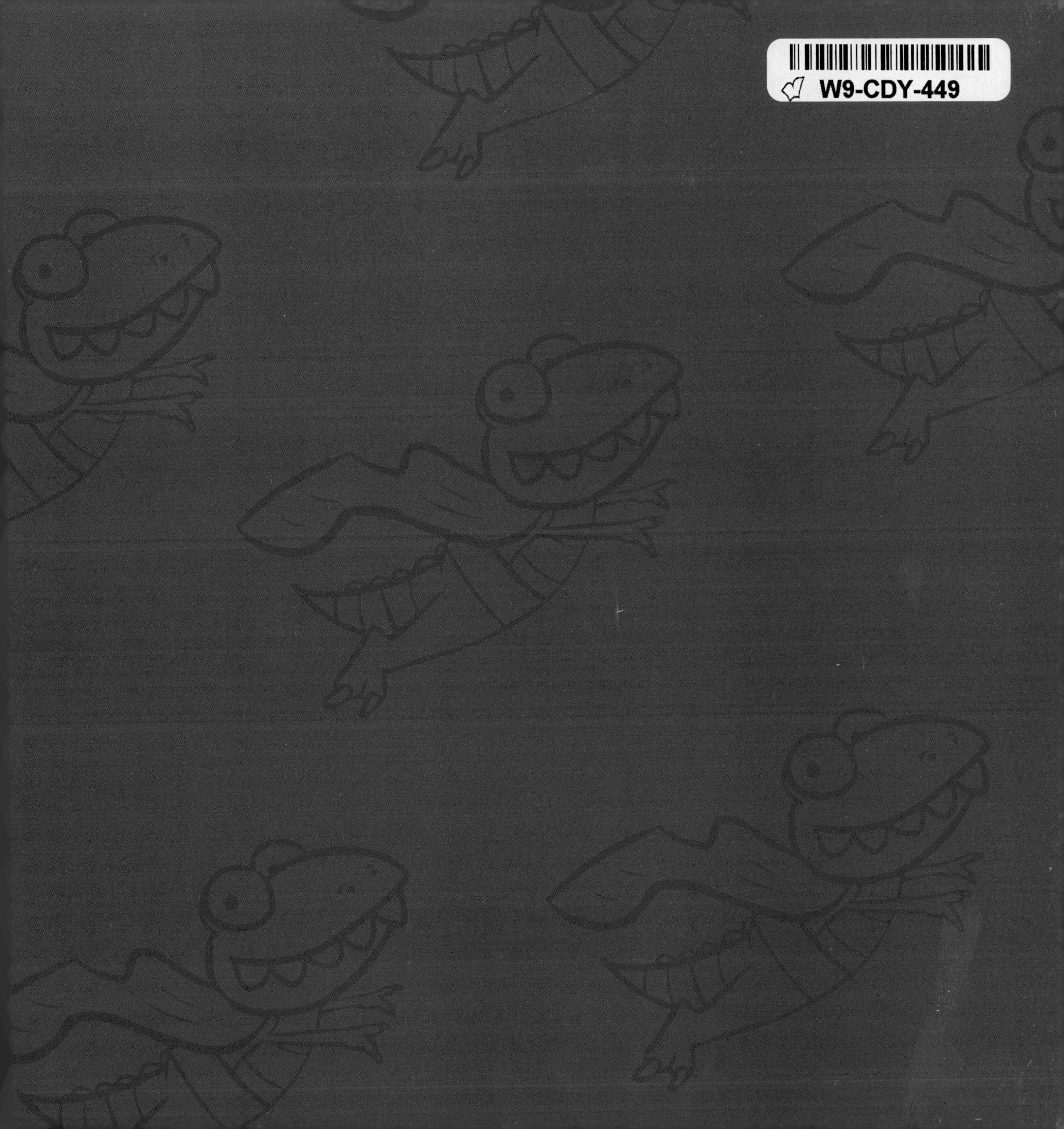

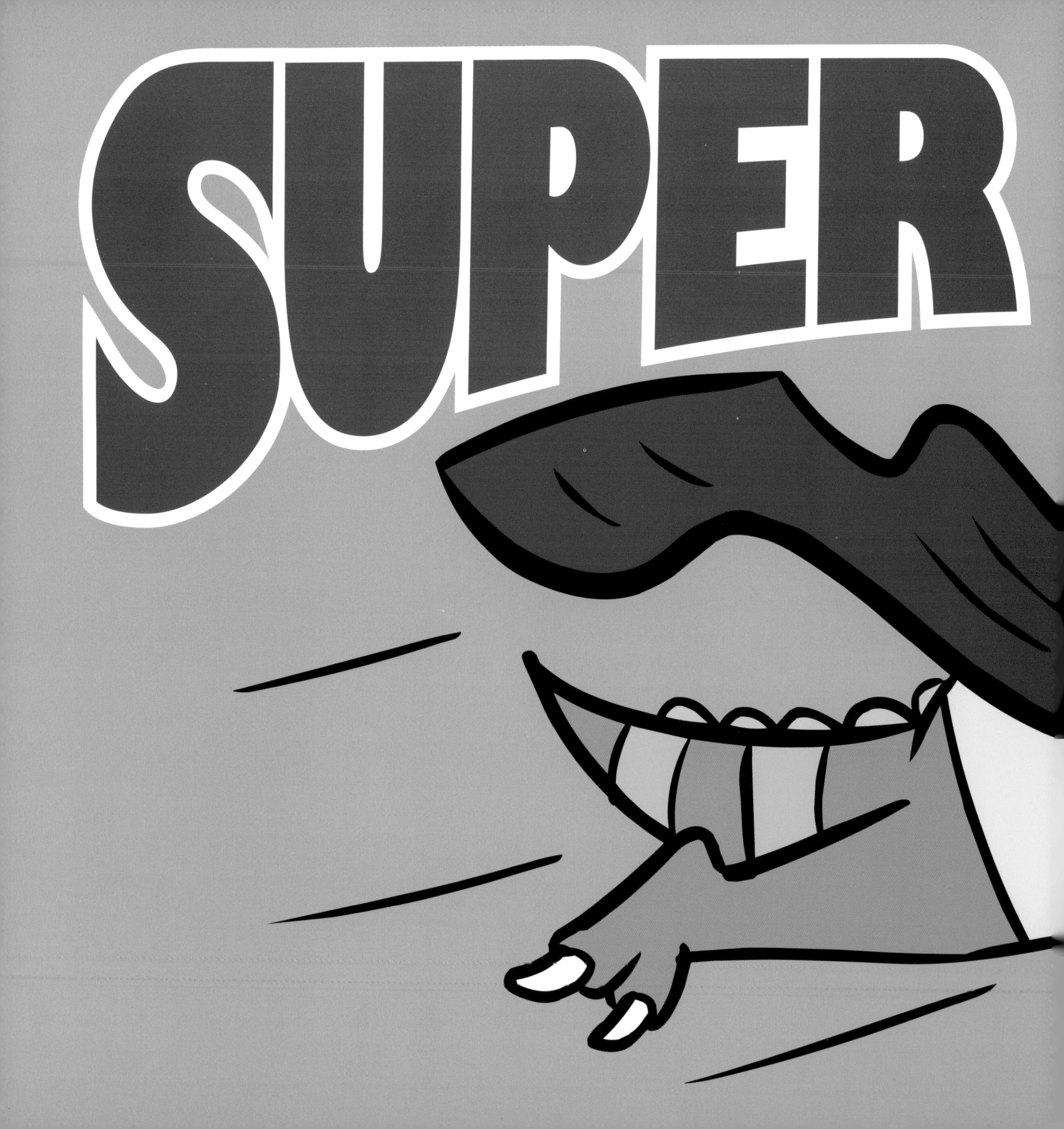
SUPER

RAWR!

Todd H. Doodler

Scholastic Press • New York

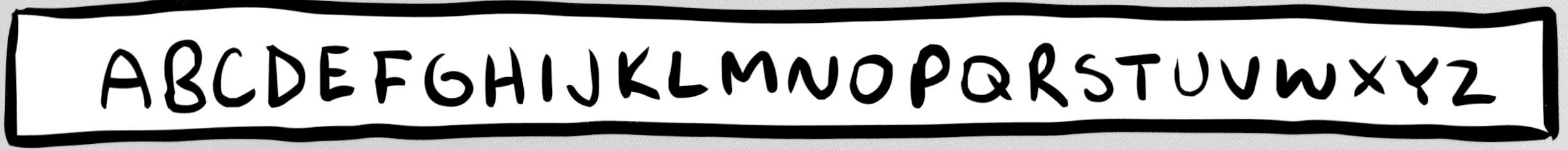
ABCDEFGHIJKLMNOPQRSTUVWXYZ

To my little dinosaur, Elle, who is my superhero! – T.D.

Library of Congress Cataloging-in-Publication Control Number: 2015027173

ISBN 978-0-545-79969-0

10 9 8 7 6 5 4 3 2 1 16 17 18 19 20

Printed in China 68 First edition, July 2016

The text was set in Burst My Bubble
The display type was set in Gill Sans Ultra Bold
Book design by Leslie Mechanic

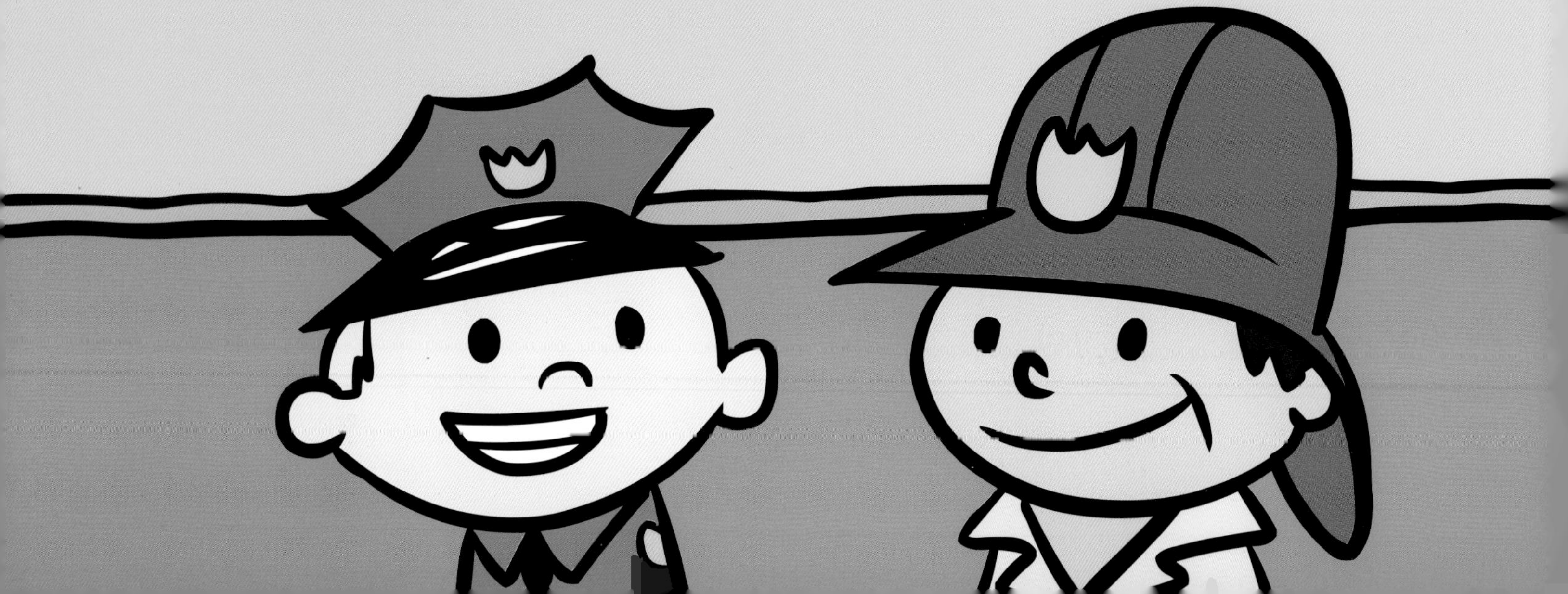

It is career day in my classroom, and it is my turn to speak.

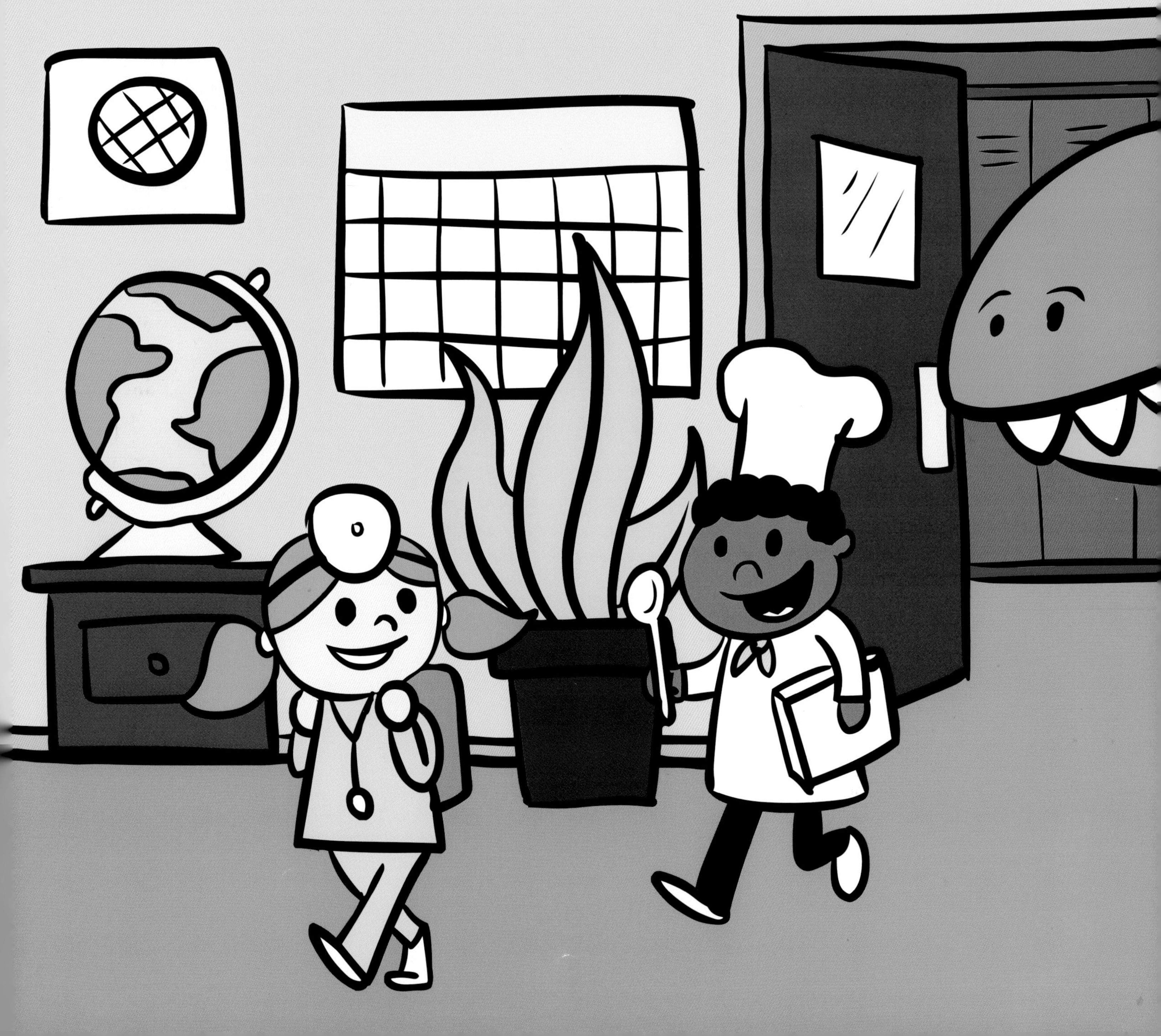

I am wearing my superhero cape and belt.

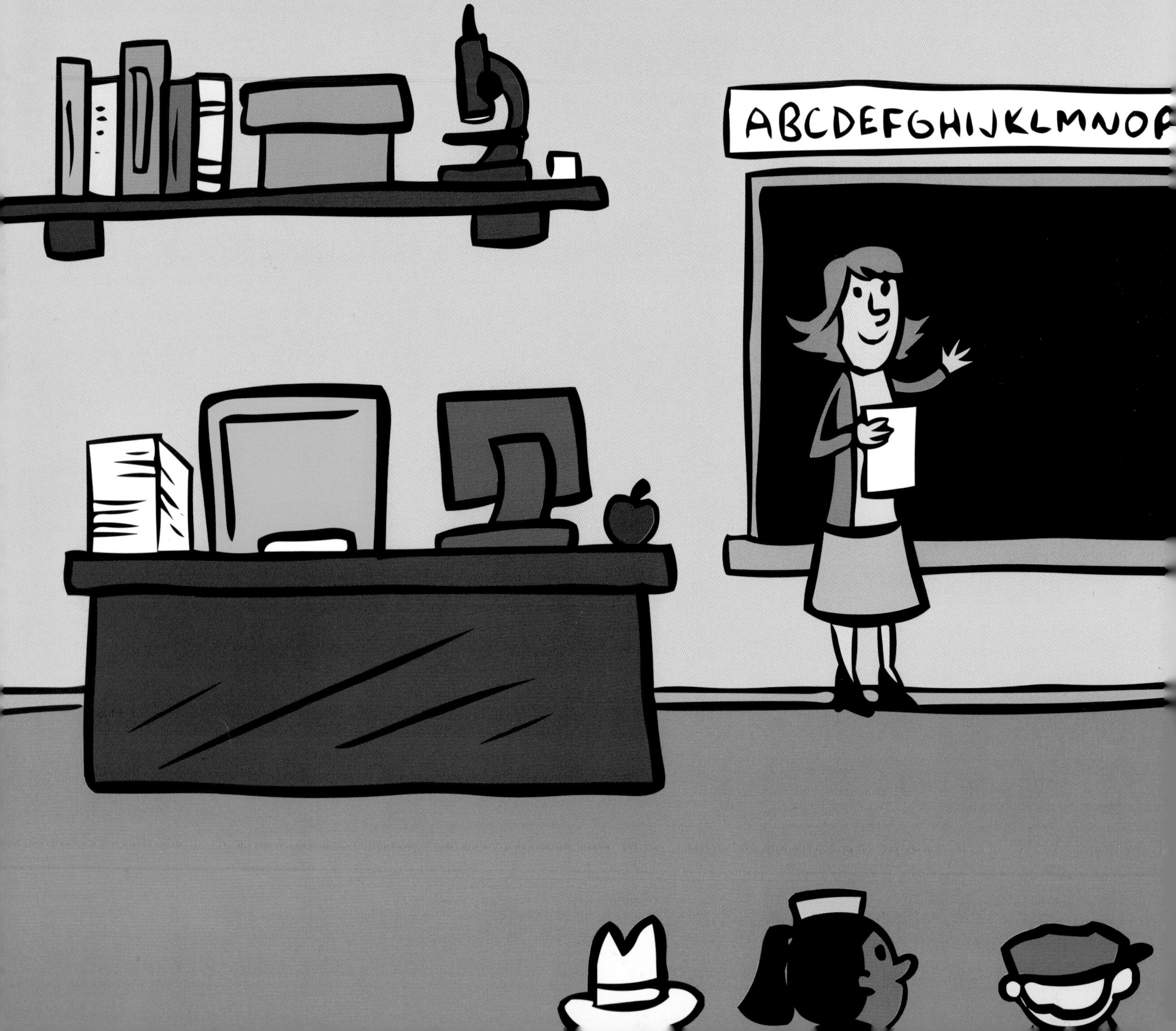
ABCDEFGHIJKLMNOP

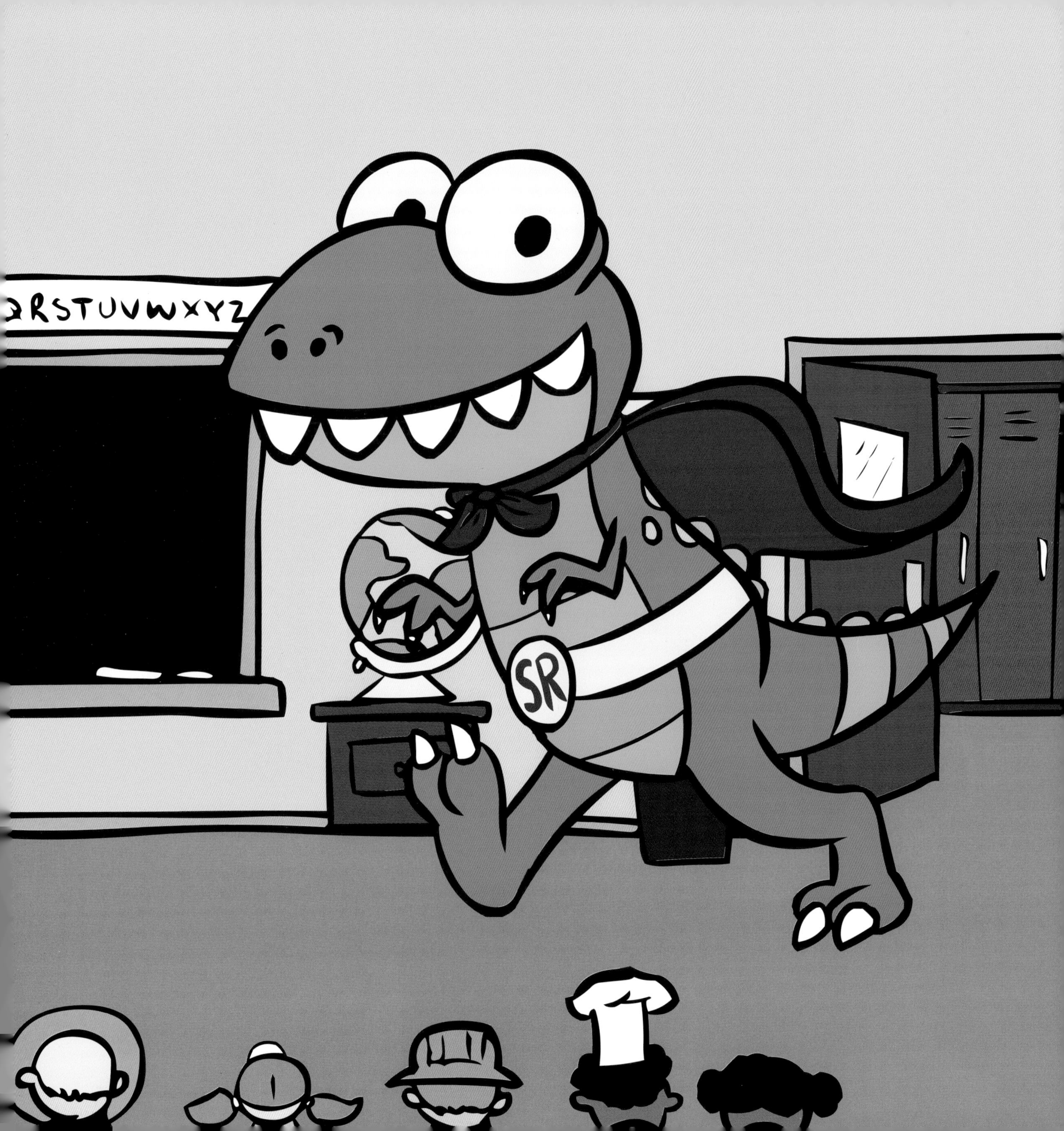
QRSTUVWXYZ
SR

Hello, I am Super Rawr,
the superhero!

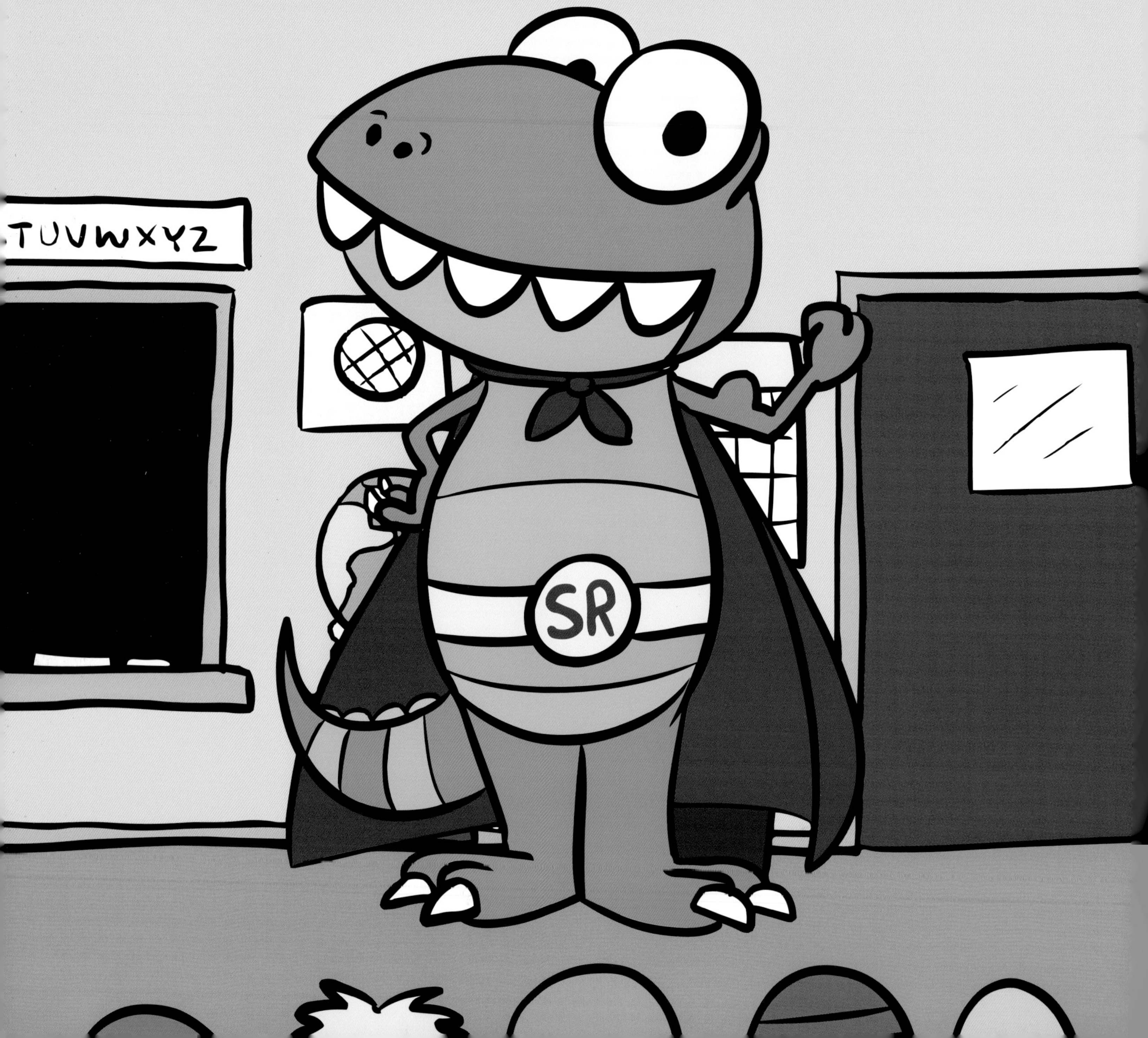
TUVWXYZ
SR

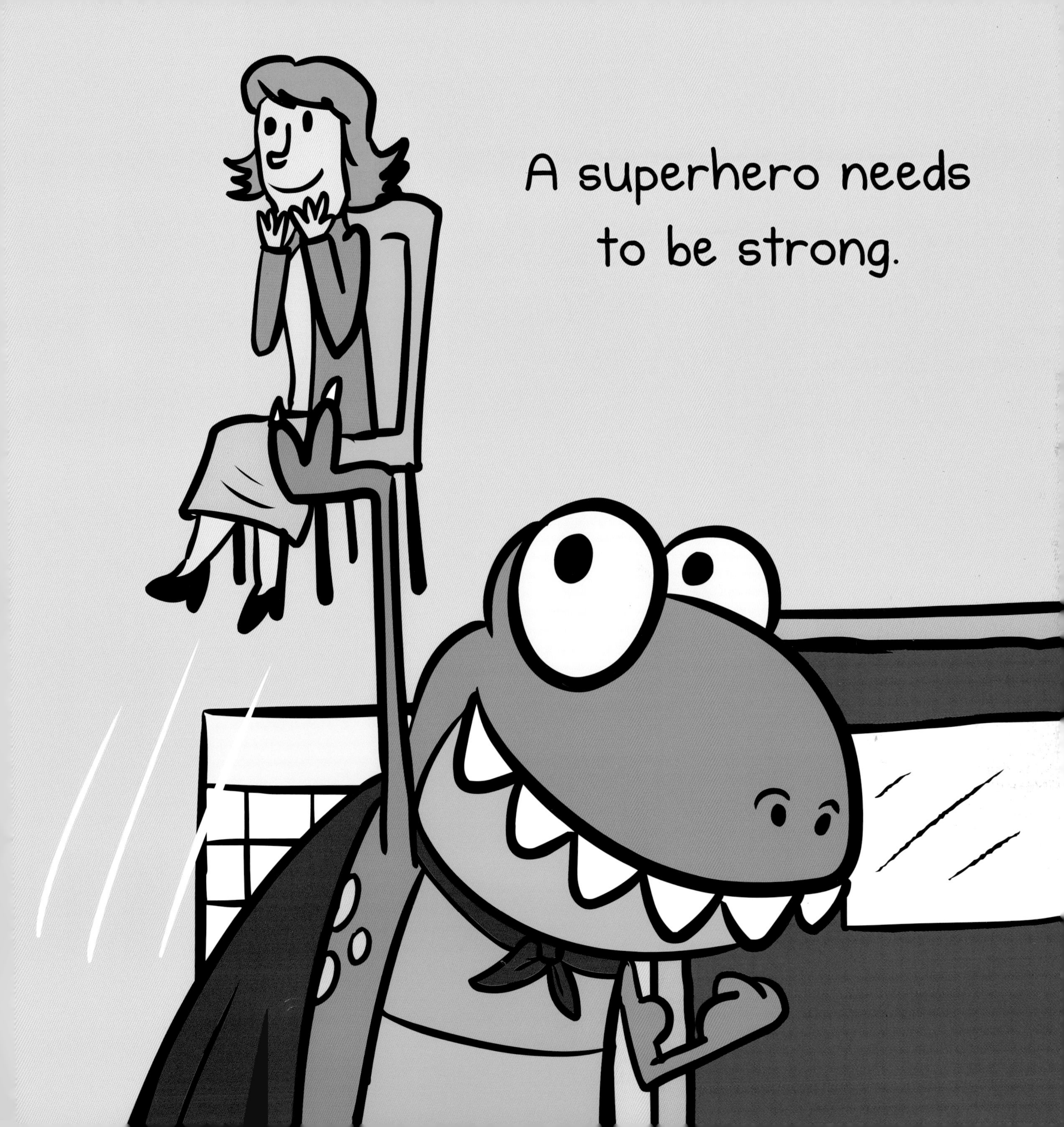
A superhero needs
to be strong.

A superhero needs to be fast.

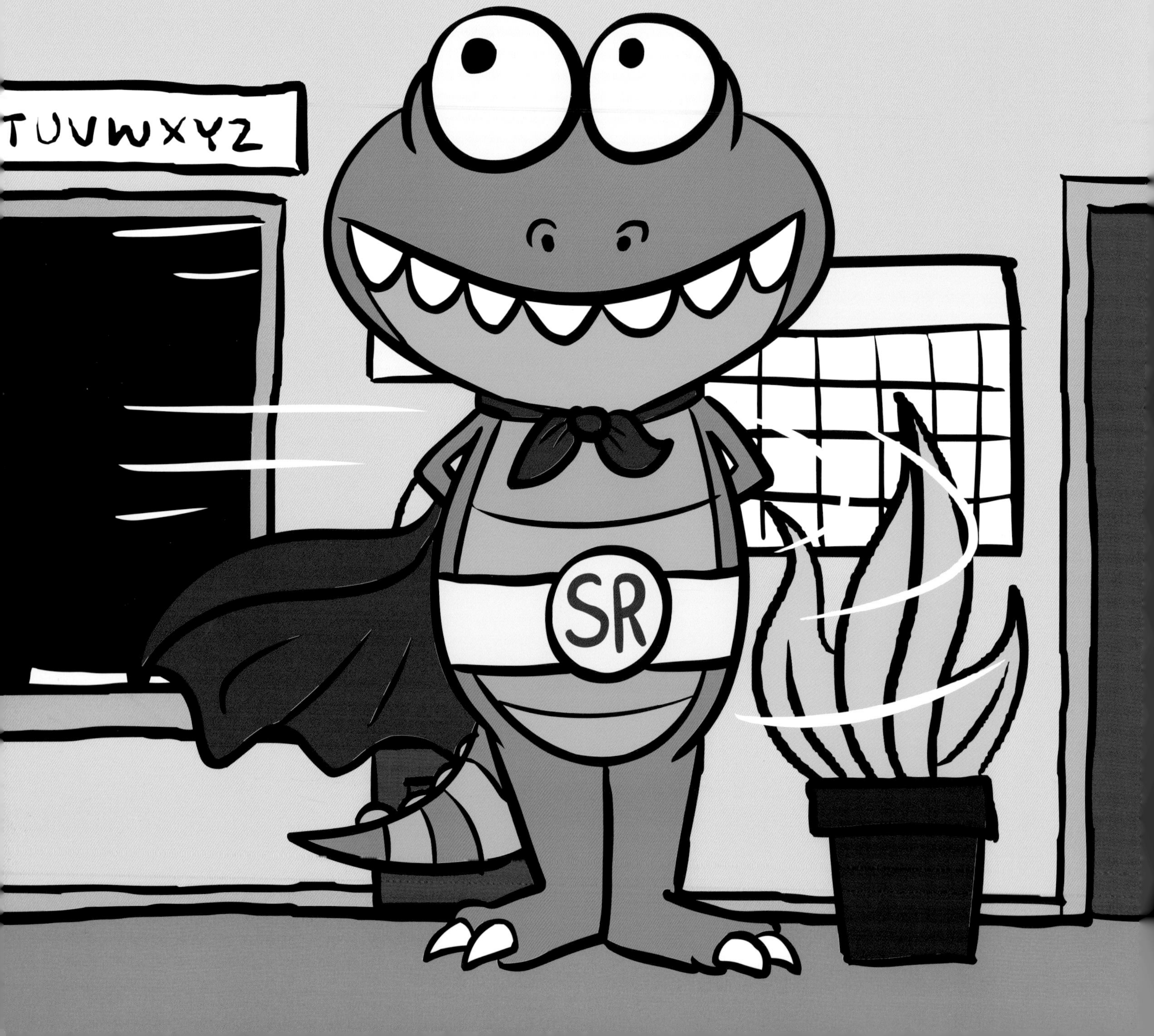

TUVWXYZ
SR

A superhero can jump over tall buildings!

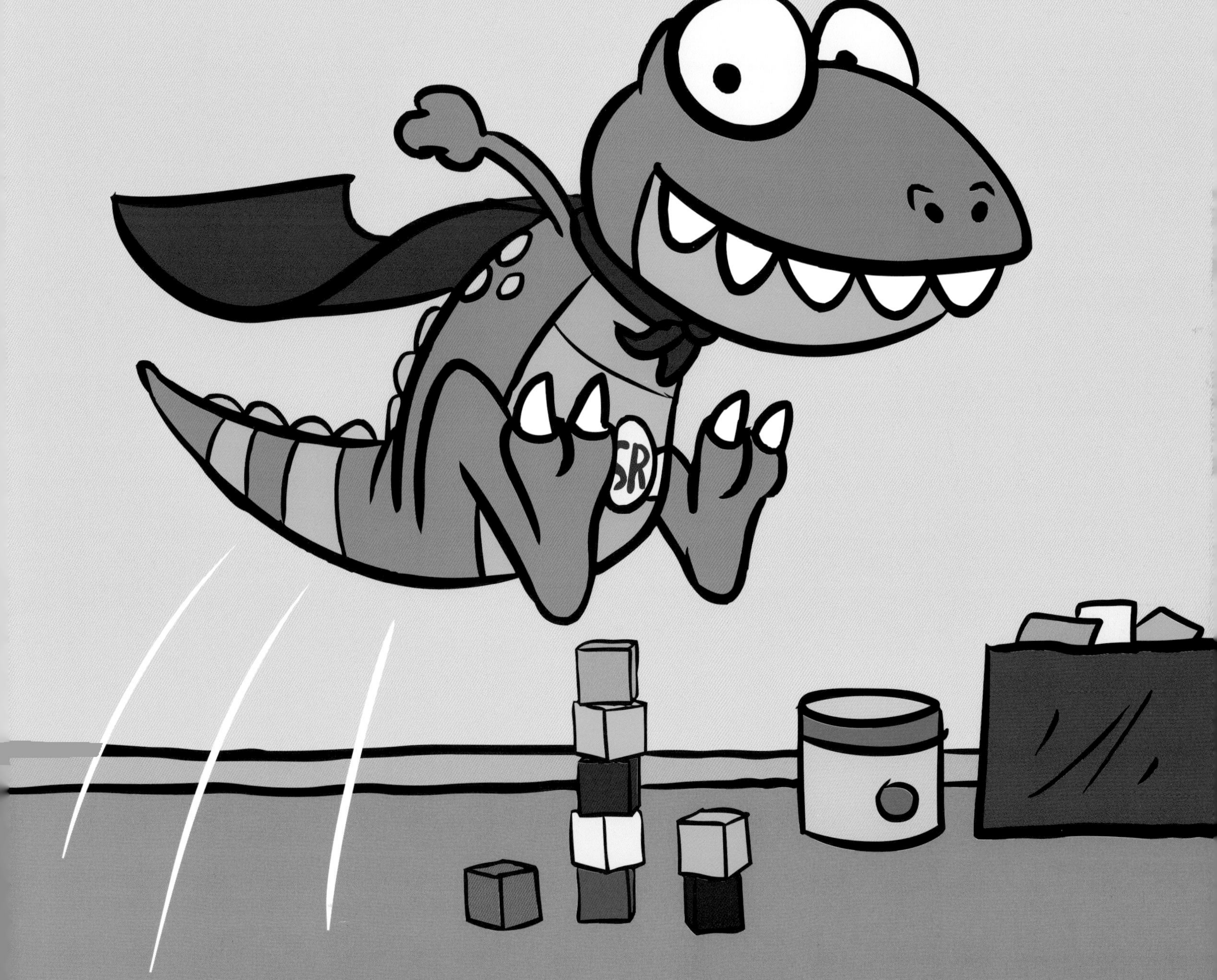
SR

A superhero can hold the world in one hand.

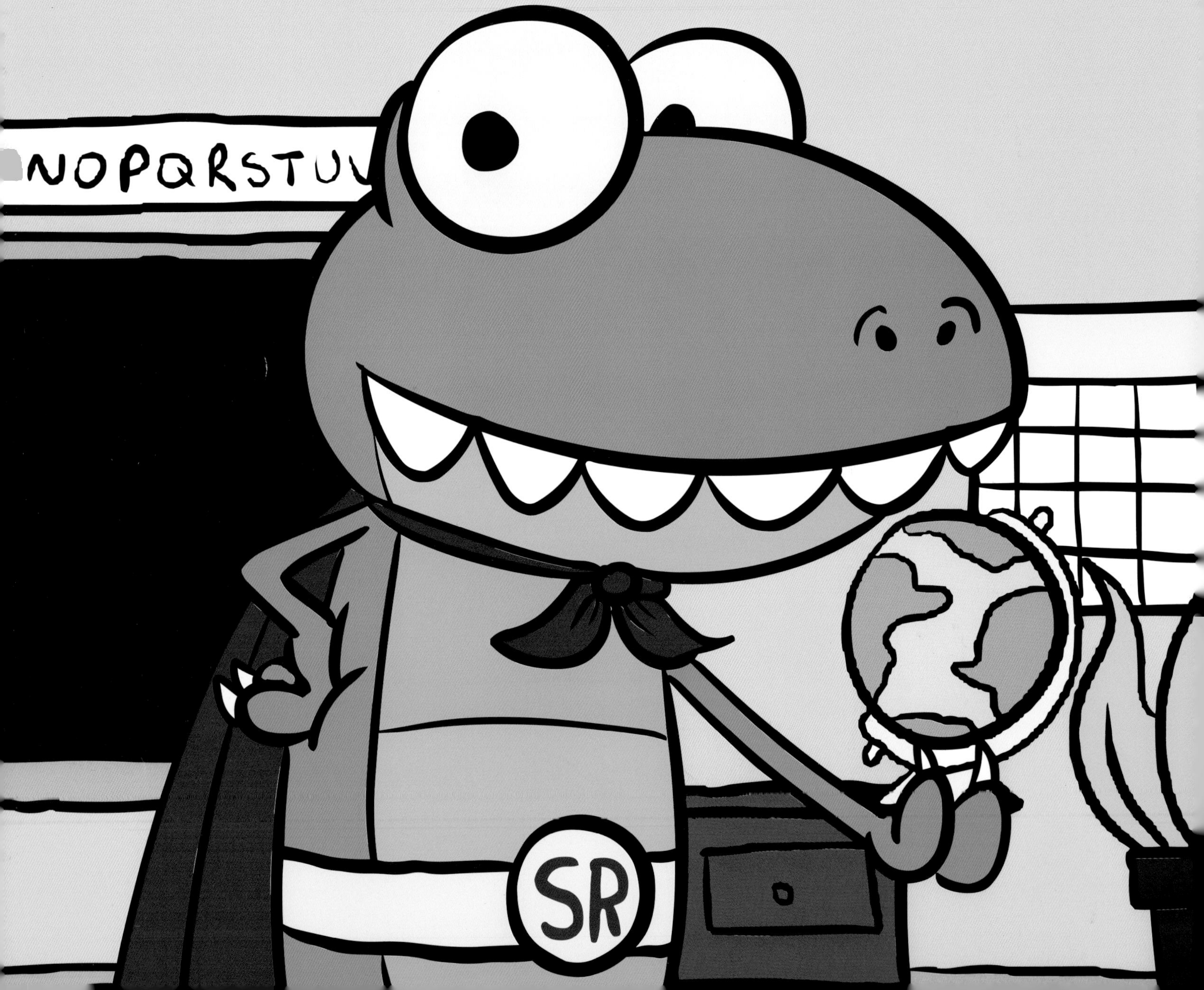
NOPQRSTU
SR

A superhero is great at hiding.

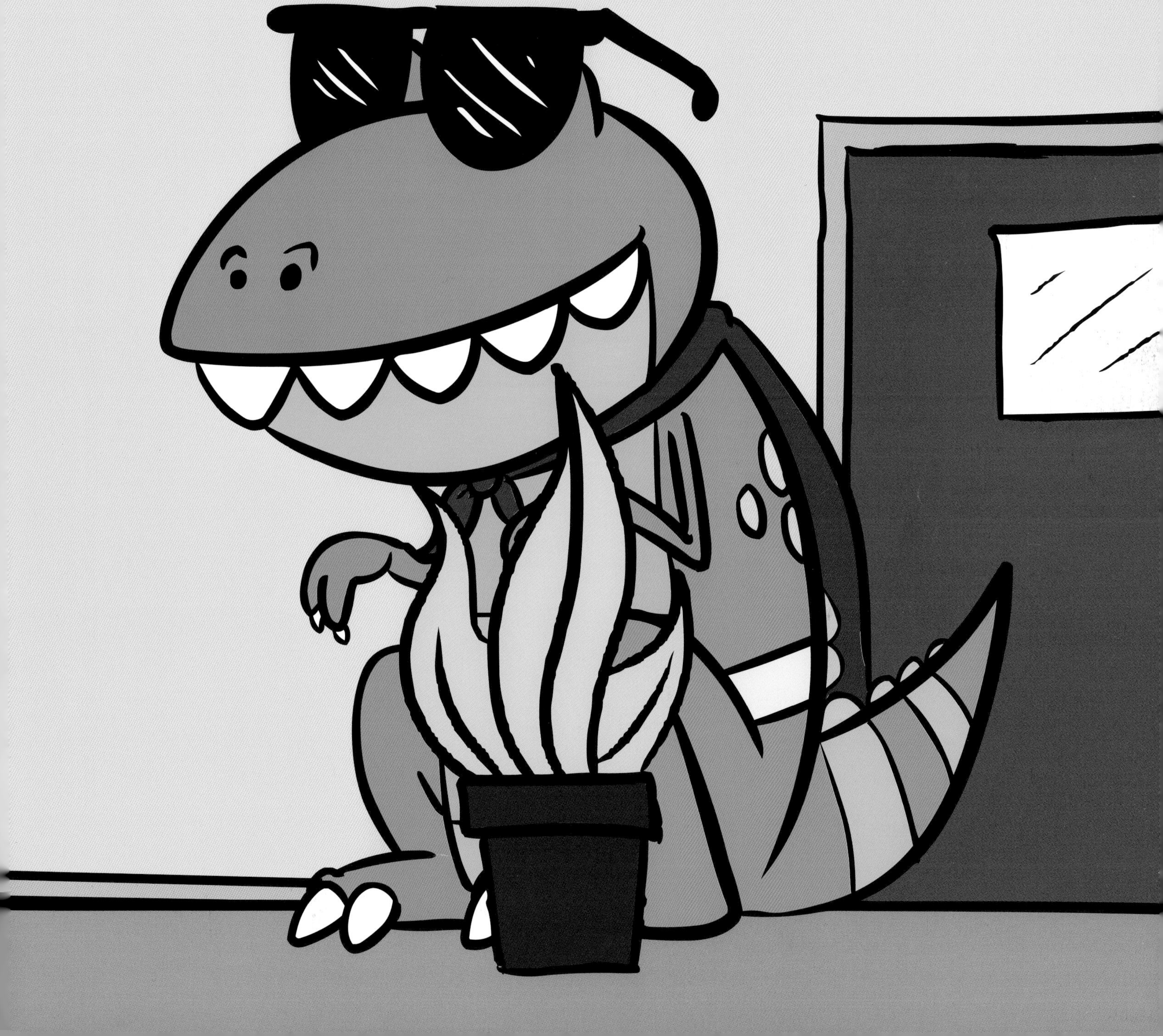

A superhero tries
his very best.

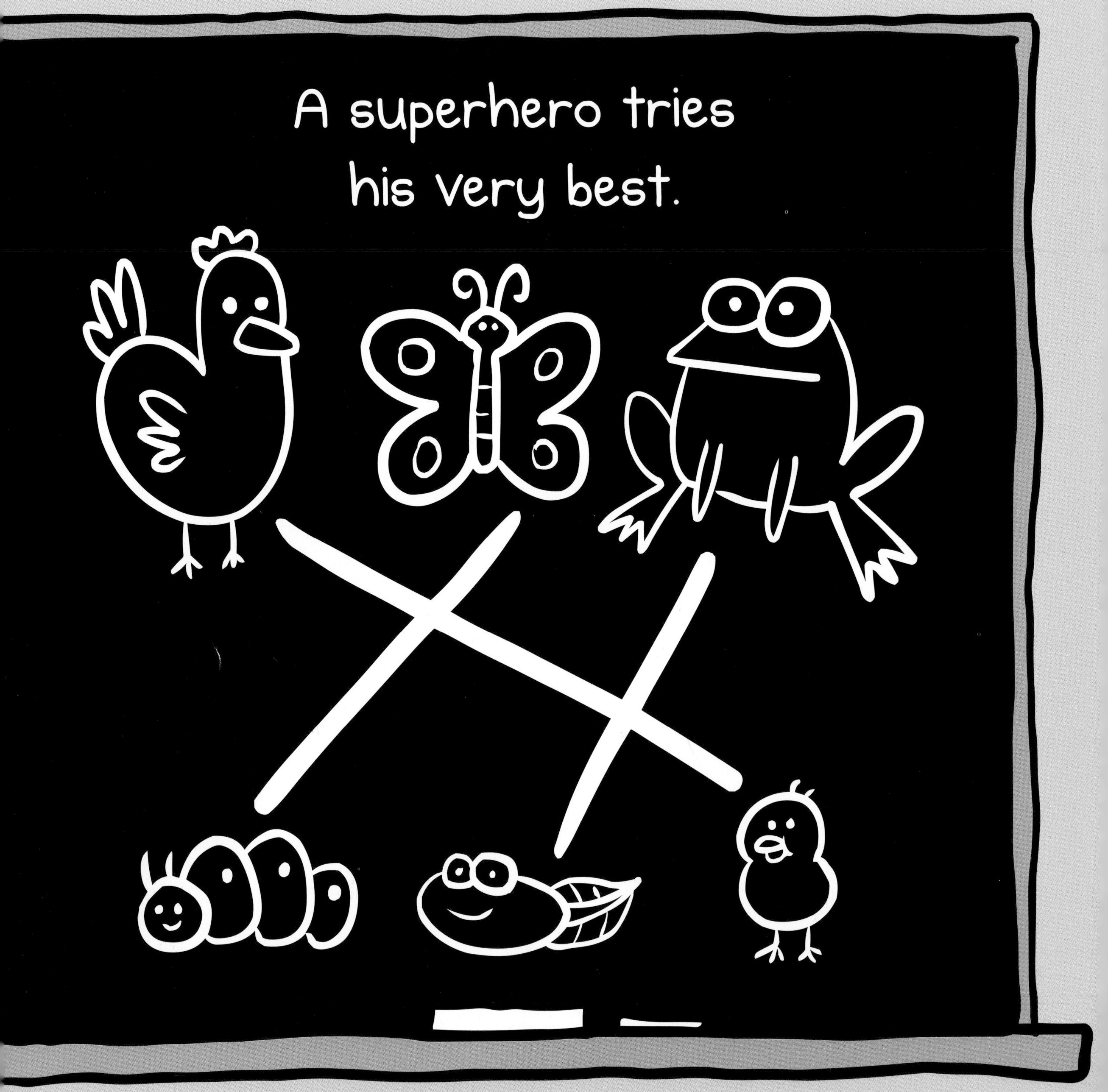

And a superhero
can fly!

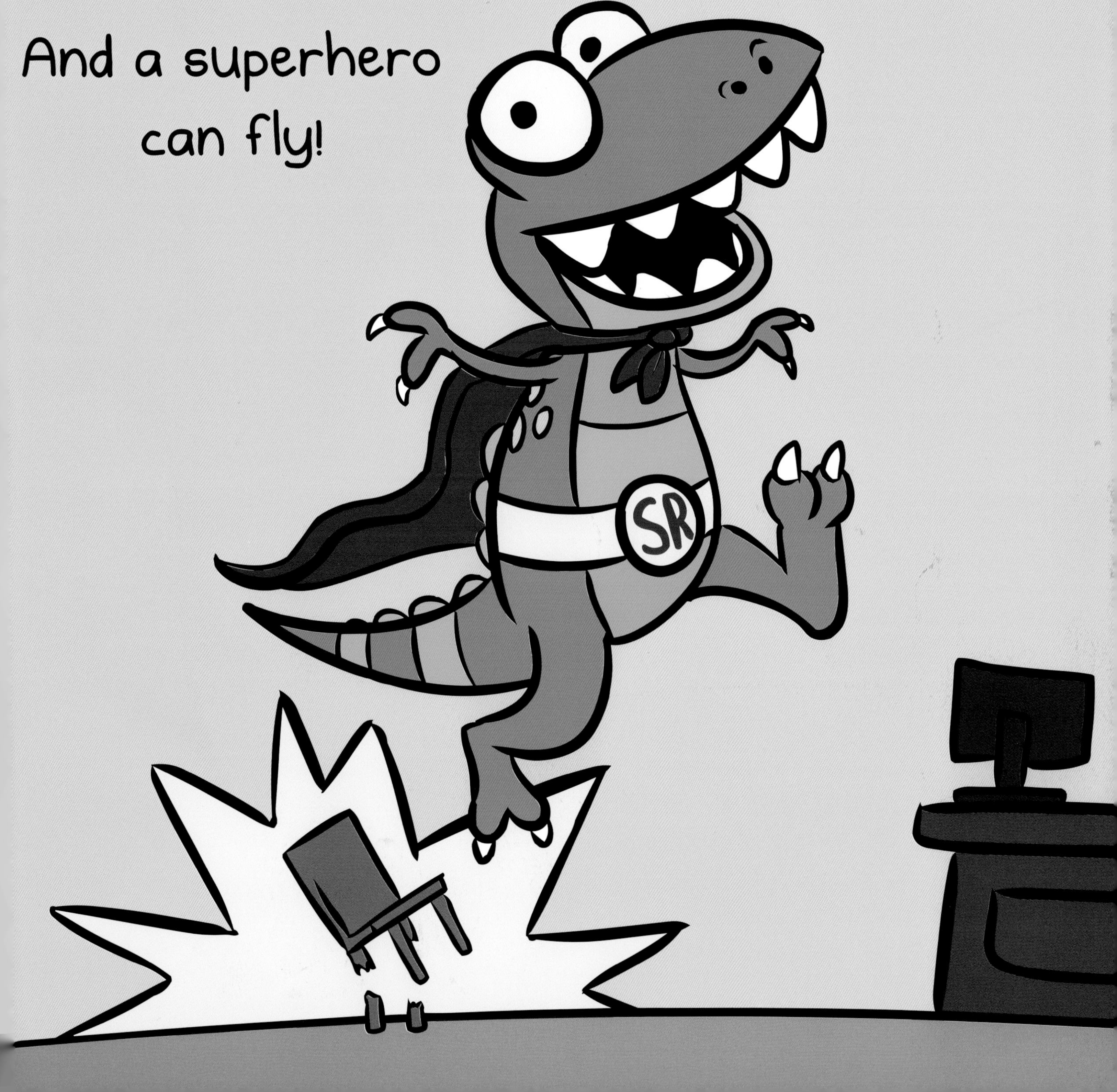
SR

I am Super Rawr, the superhero!
Thank you.

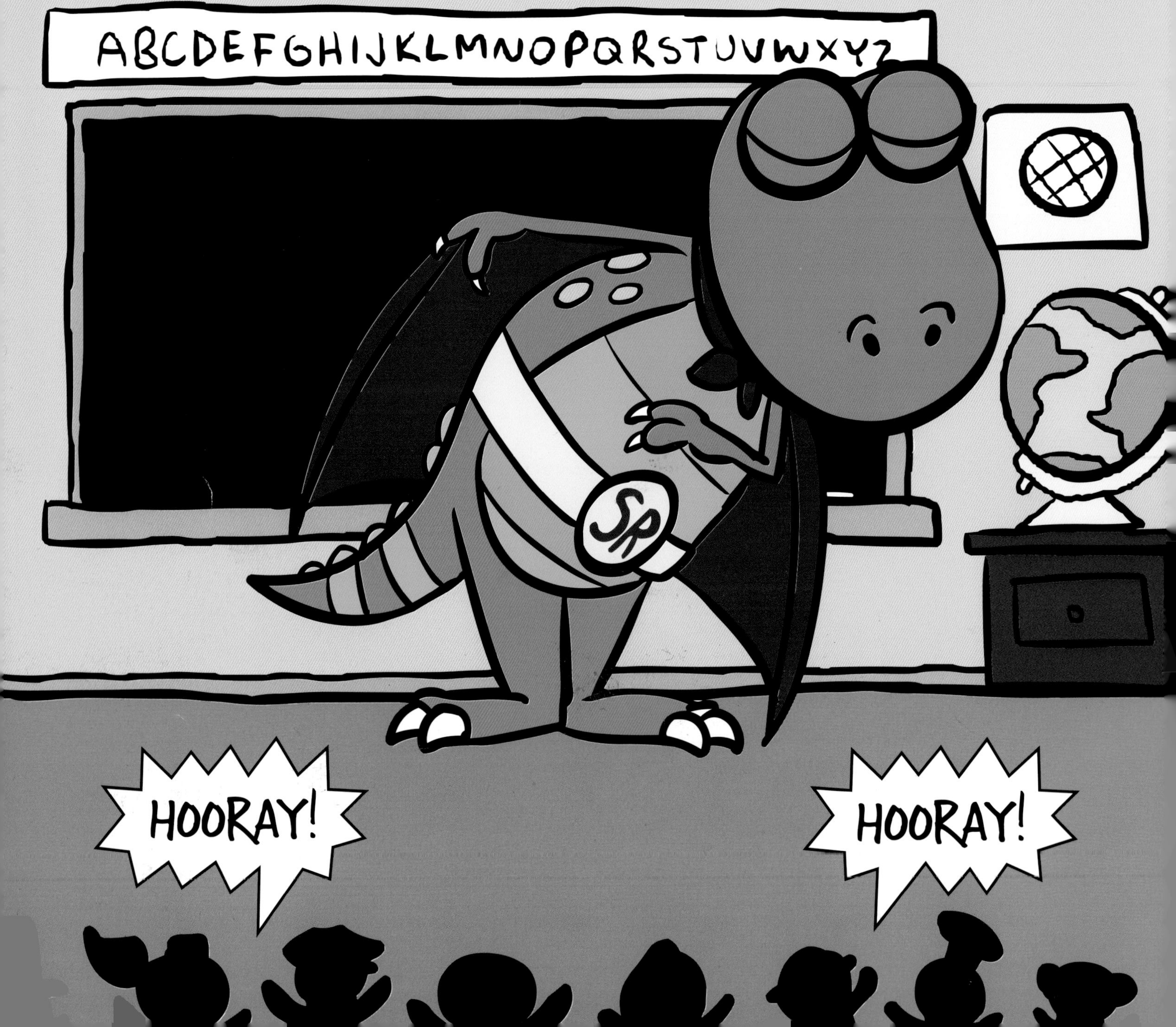
ABCDEFGHIJKLMNOPQRSTUVWXYZ
SR
HOORAY!
HOORAY!

After school, everyone goes to the playground.

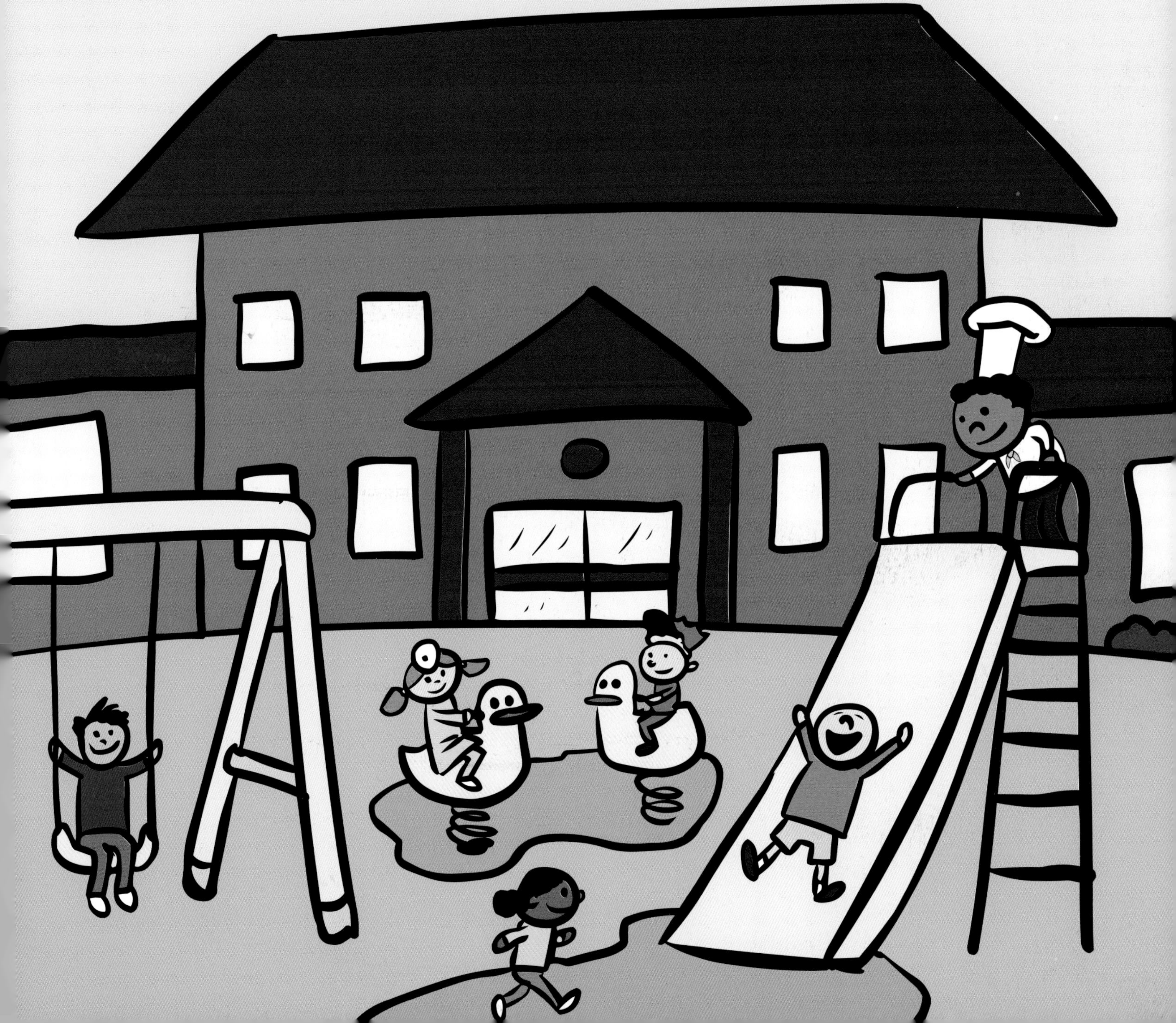

A fire hydrant is broken and spraying water everywhere.

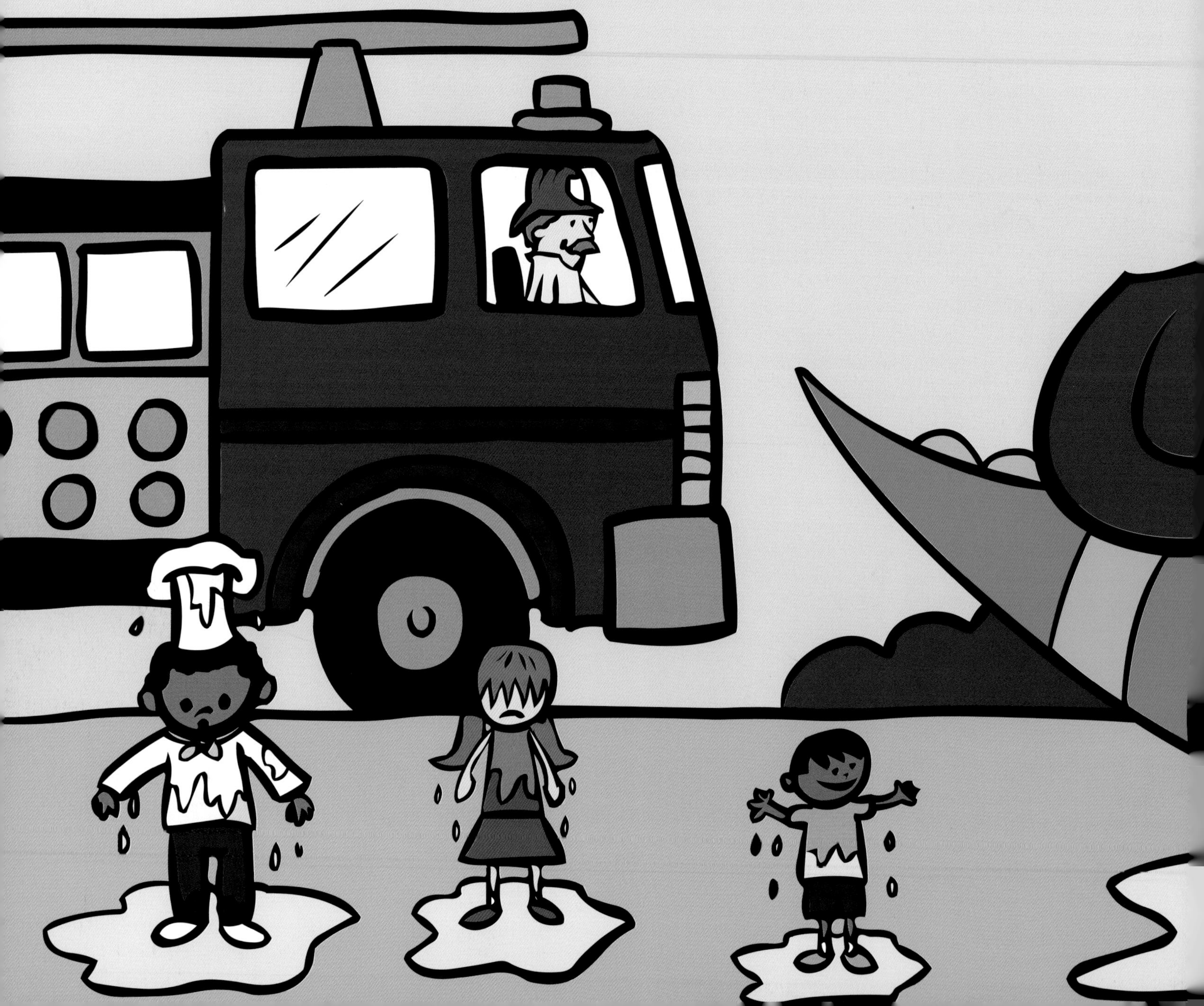

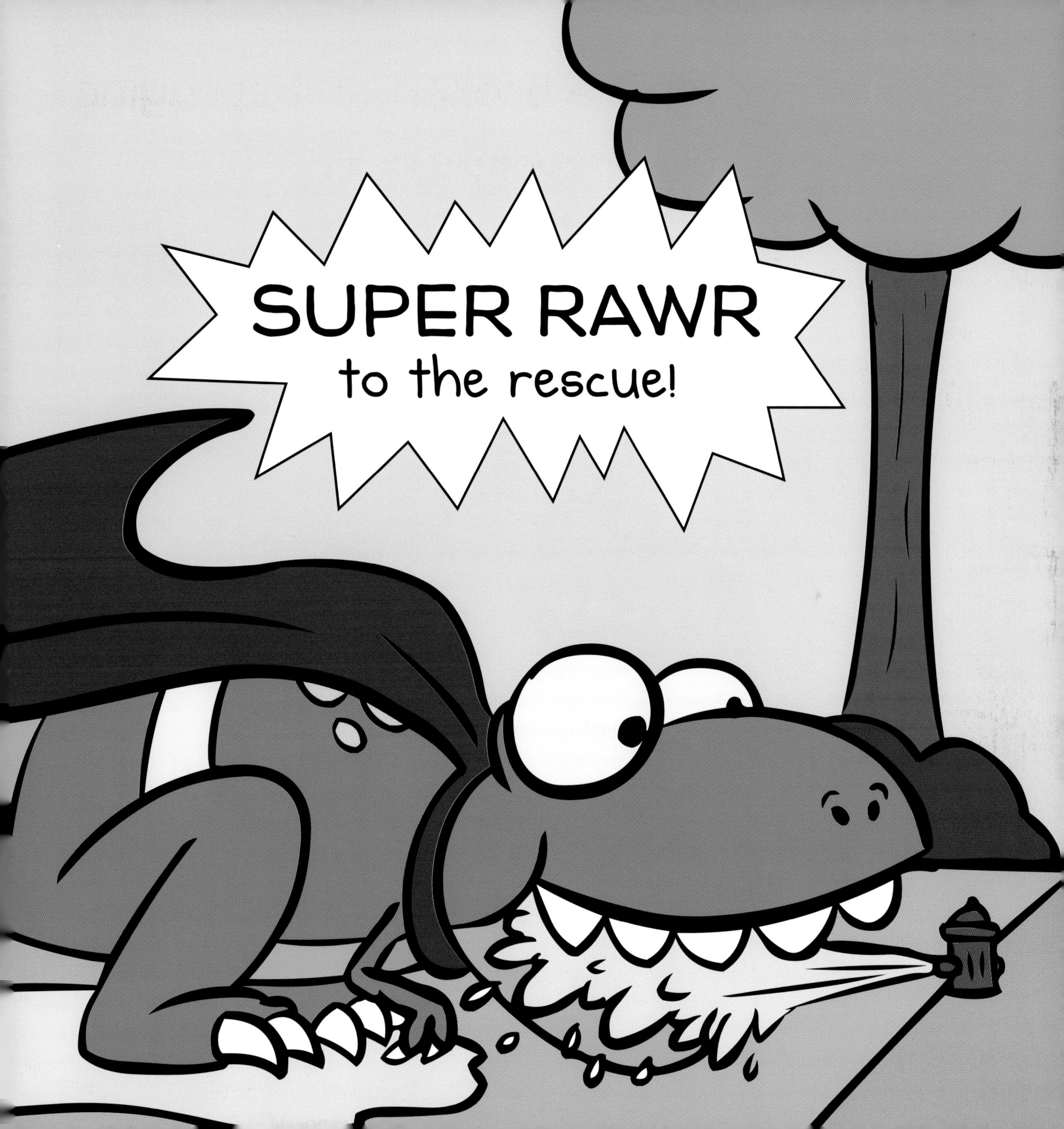
SUPER RAWR
to the rescue!

A kitten is trapped up in a tree.

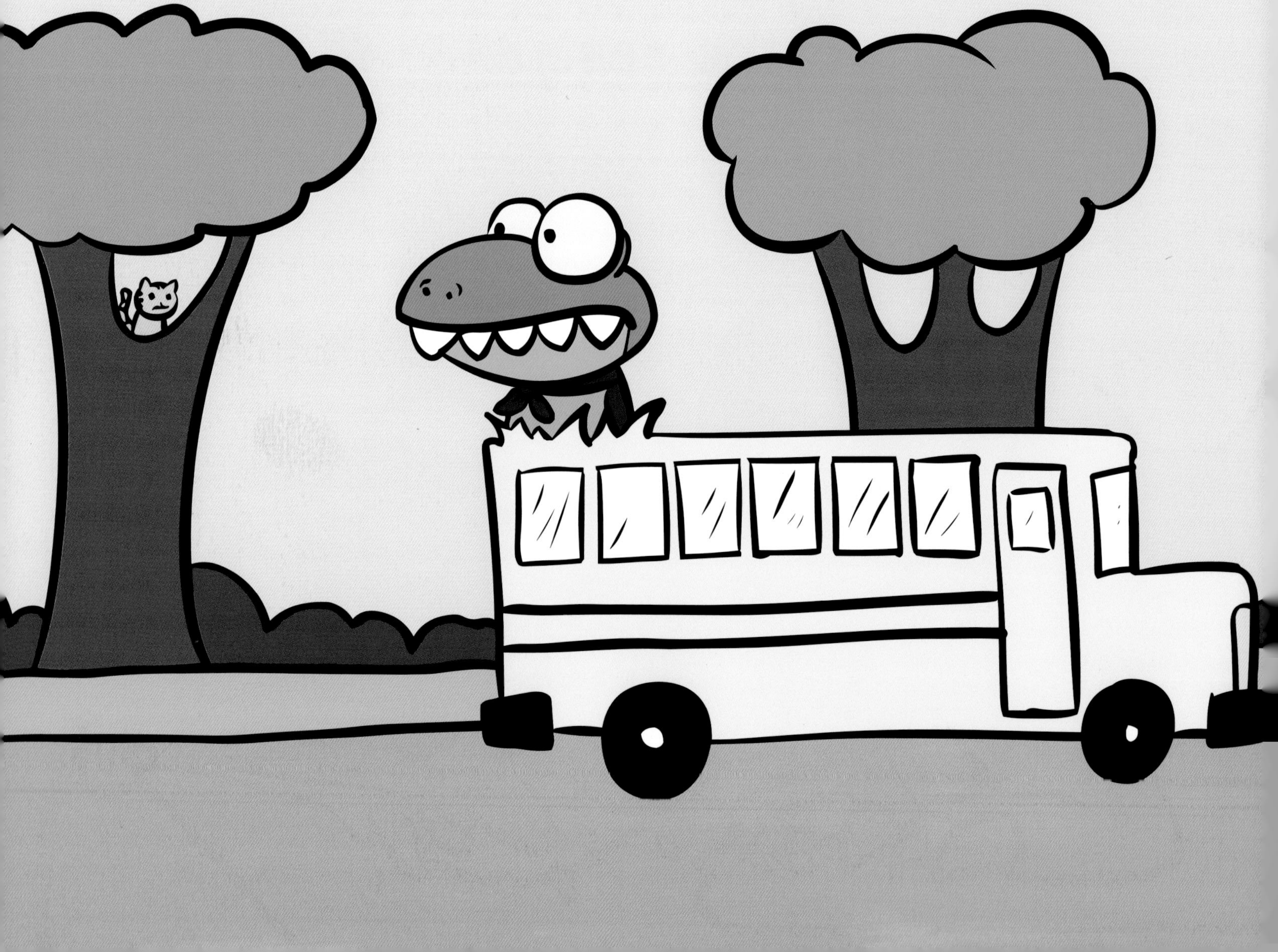

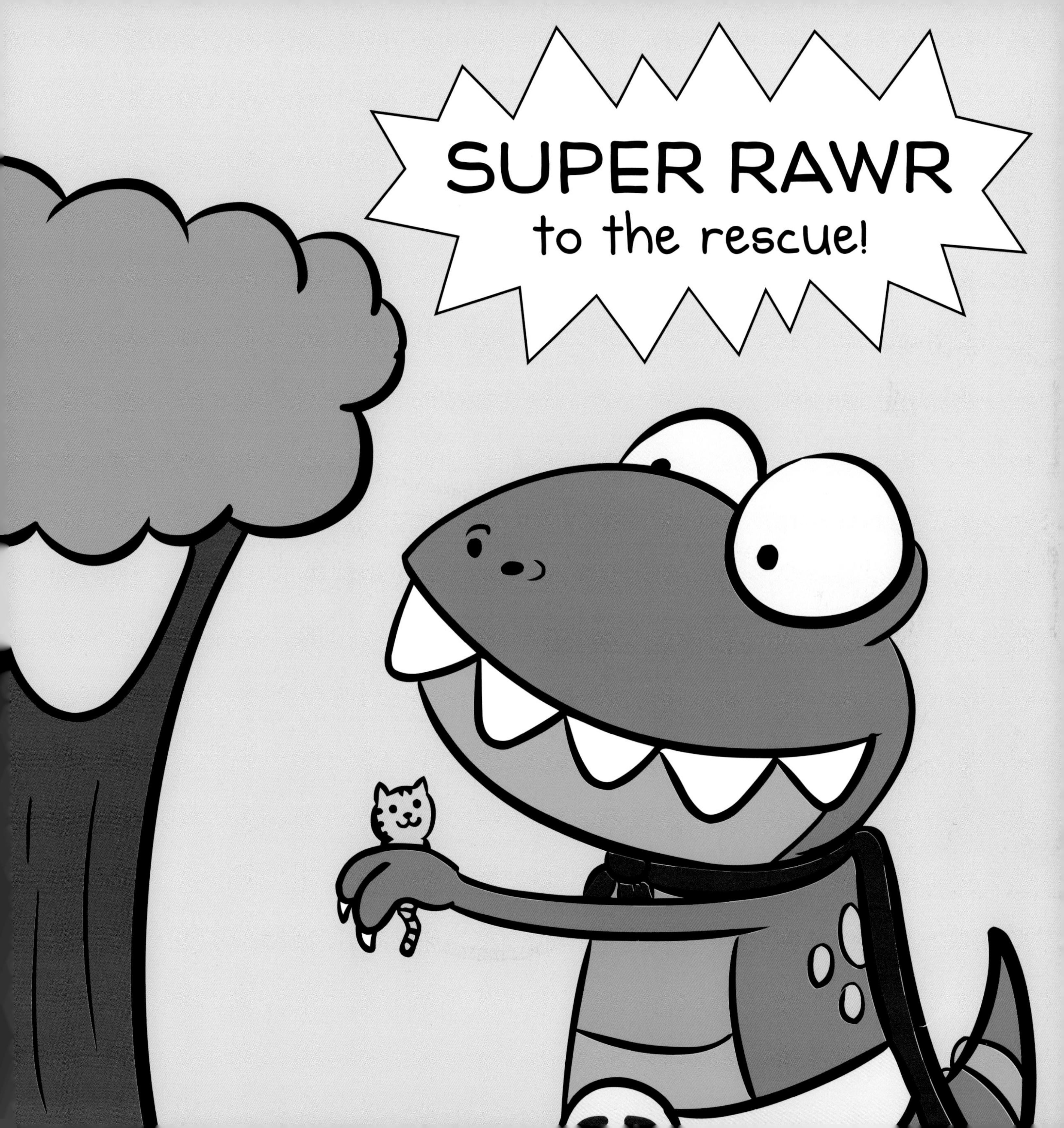
SUPER RAWR
to the rescue!

I love being a superhero,

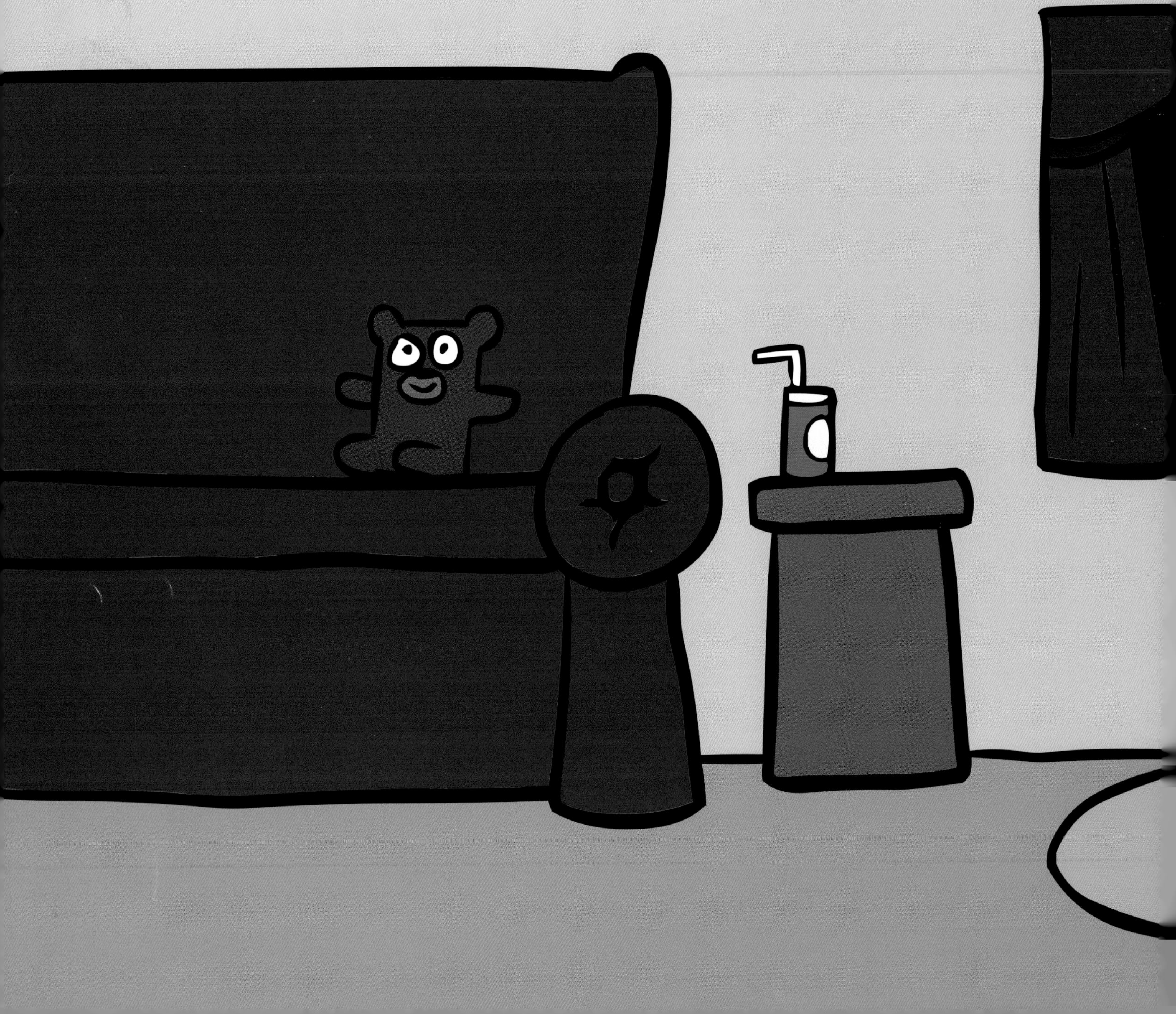

but sometimes it is exhausting.

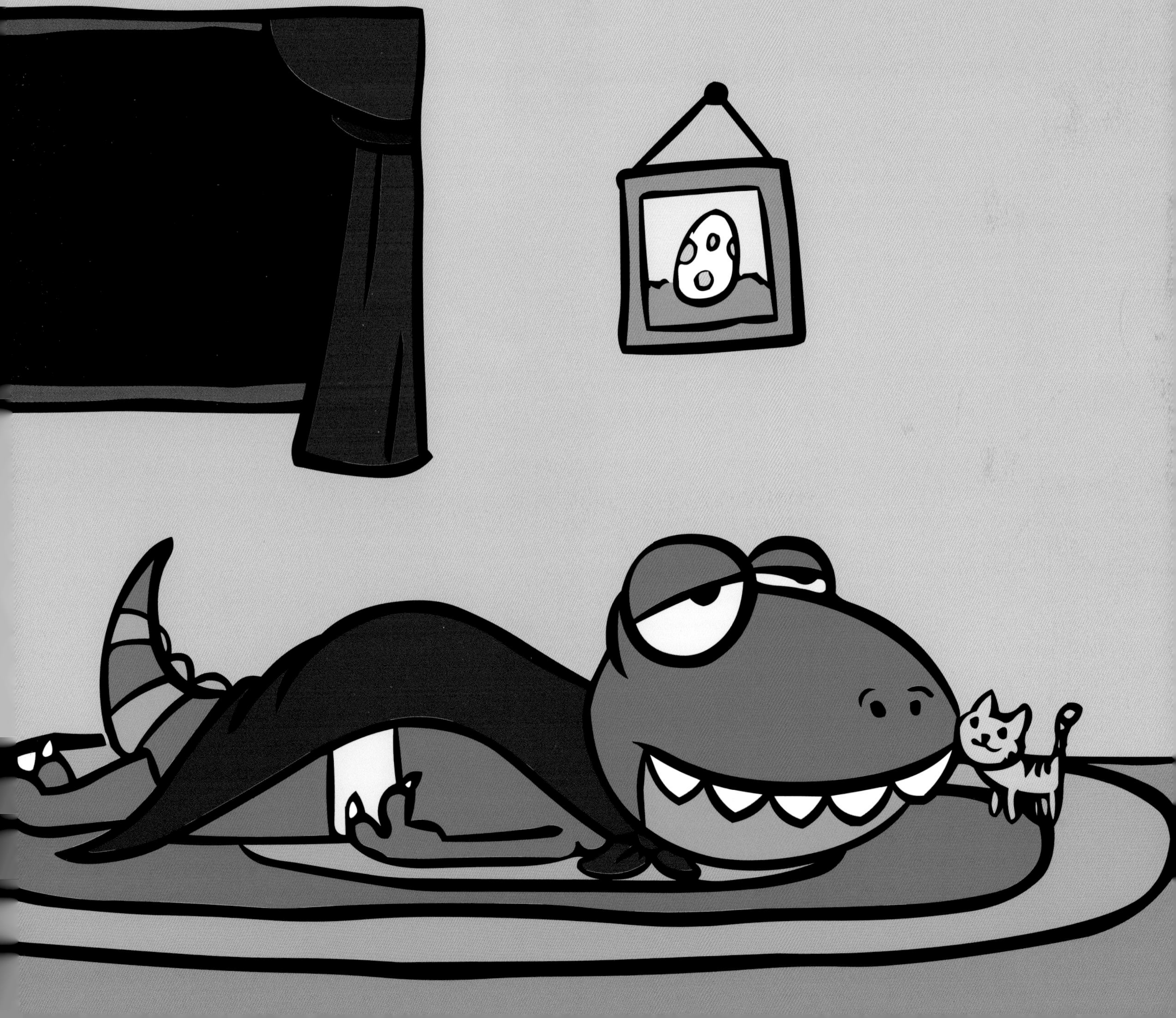

I love being a dinosaur even more!

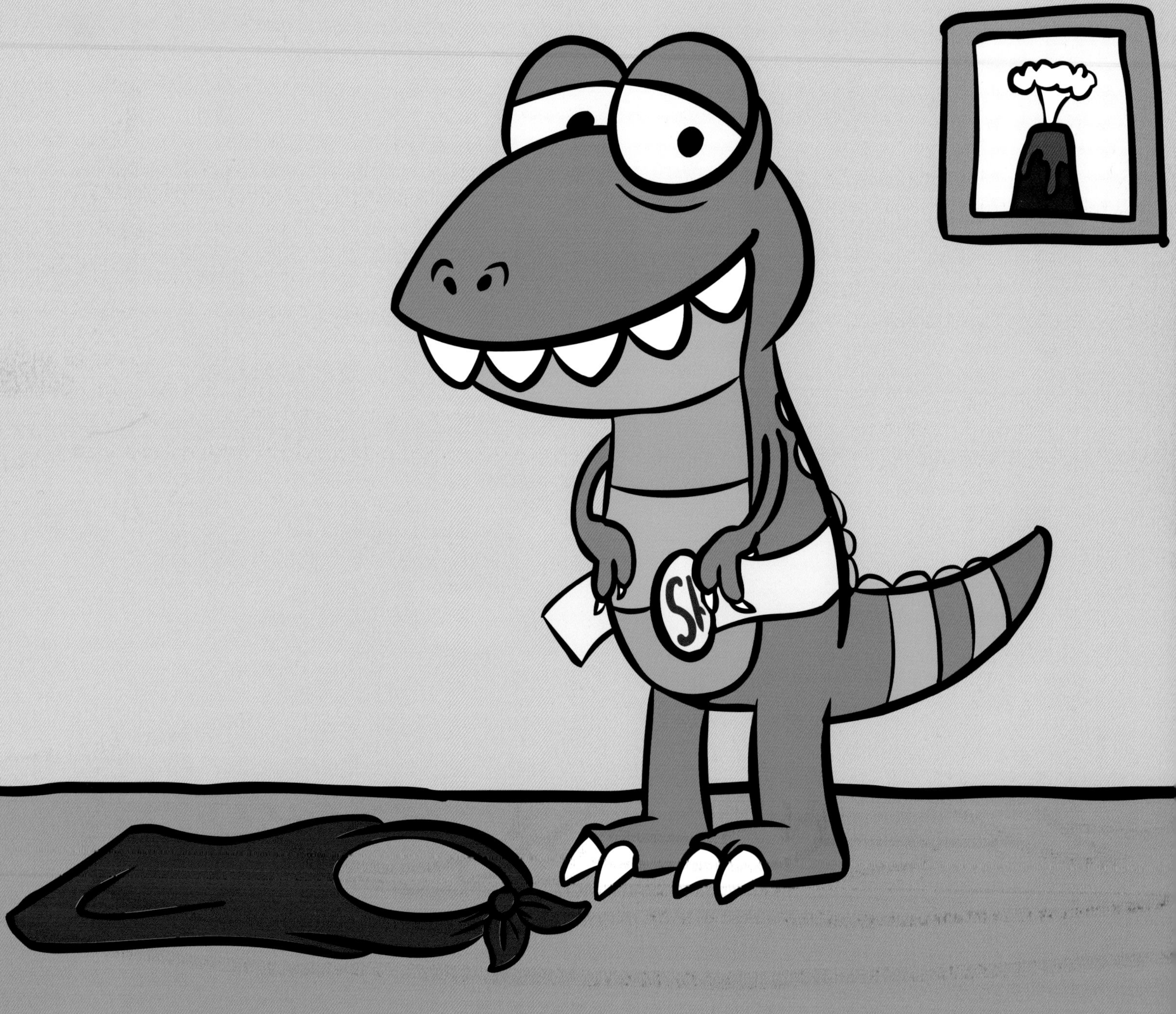

Maybe one day I'll be an astronaut!

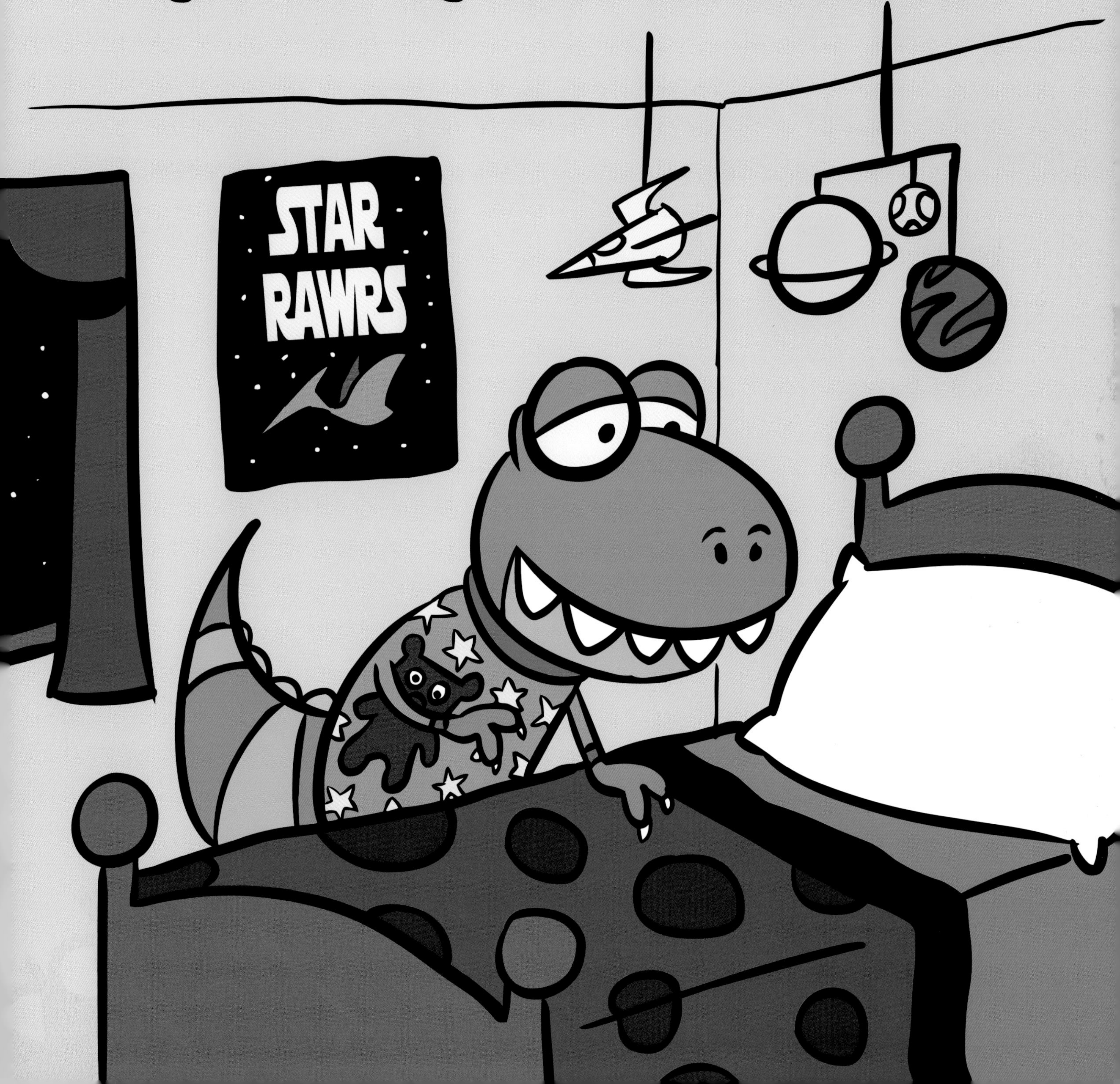

STAR RAWRS

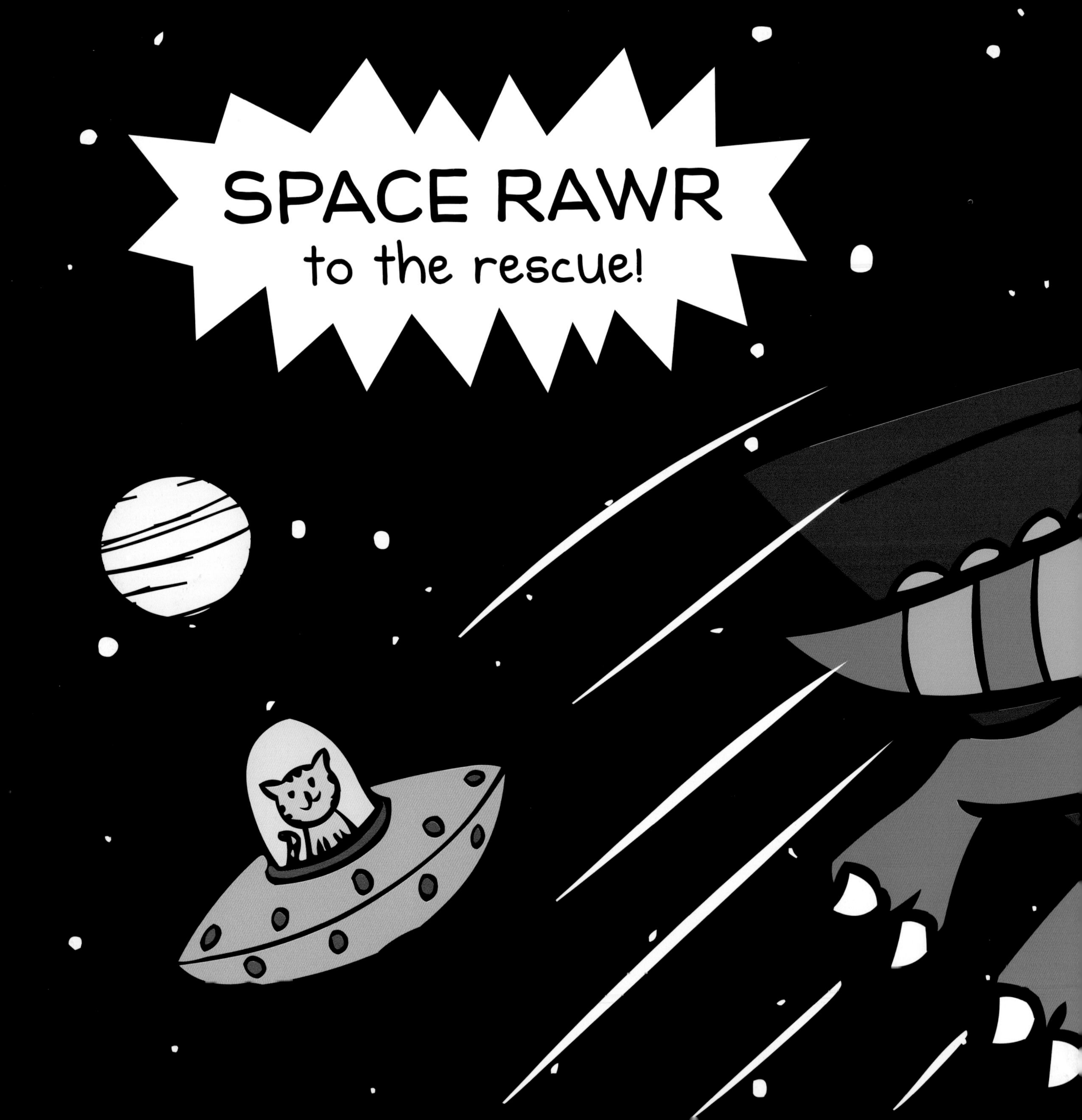
SPACE RAWR
to the rescue!

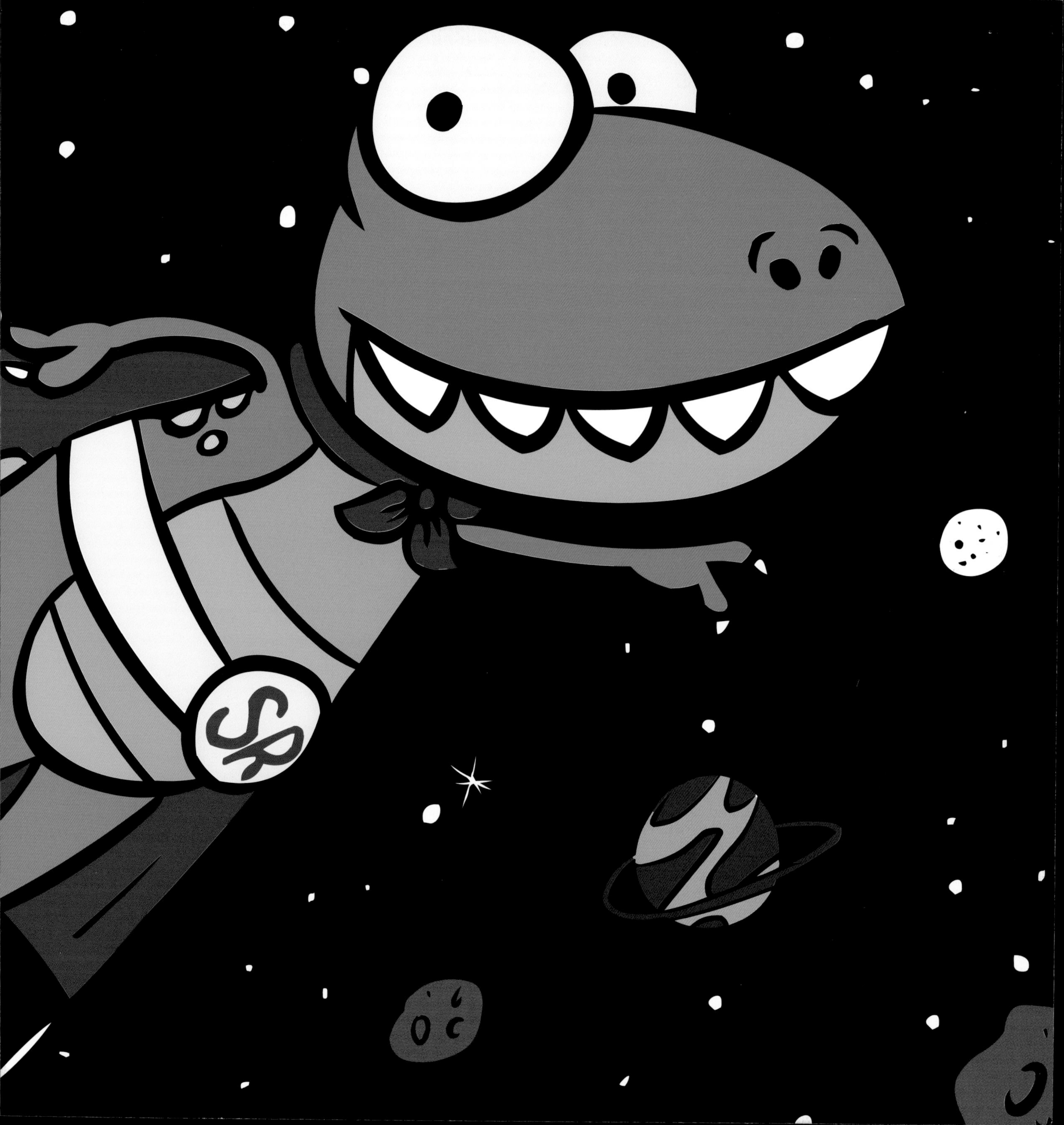
SR

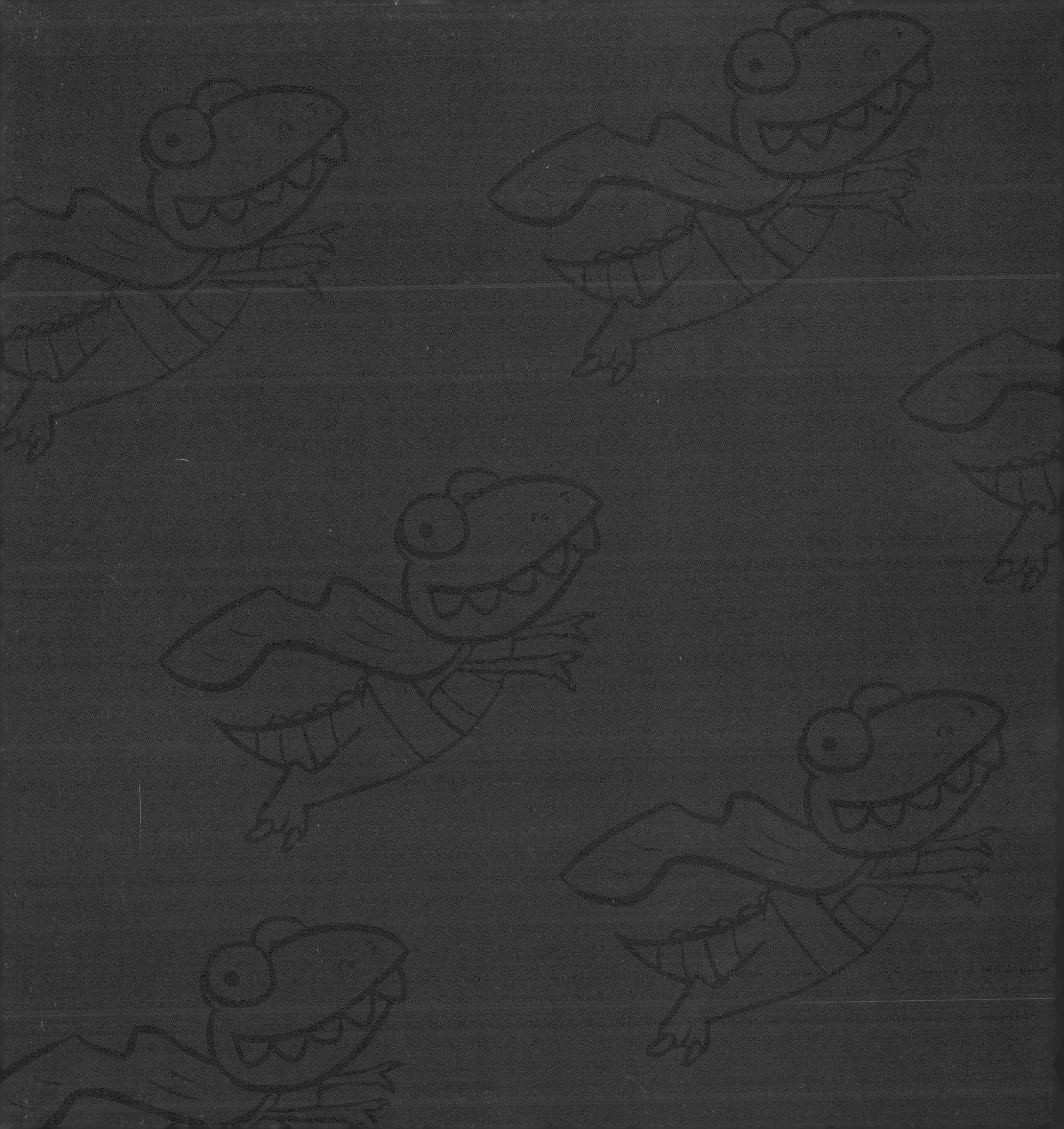